MIND OVER MATTER

SUPER HUMAN

MIND OVER MATTER

R. T. MARTIN

darbycreek

MINNEAPOLIS

Darby Creek
A division of Lerner Publishing Group, Inc.
241 First Avenue North
Minneapolis, MN 55401 USA

For reading levels and more information, look up this title at www.lernerbooks.com.

The images in this book are used with the permission of: iStock.com/Vladimirovic; iStock.com/tolokonov; iStock.com/monsitj; iStock.com/edge69; iStock.com/sinemaslow.

Main body text set in Janson Text LT Std 12/17.5.
Typeface provided by Adobe Systems.

Library of Congress Cataloging-in-Publication Data

Names: Martin, R. T., 1988– author.
Title: Mind over matter / R.T. Martin.
Description: Minneapolis : Darby Creek, [2018] | Series: Superhuman | Summary: On his sixteenth birthday, Parker, once a loner, discovers he has the power of telekinesis and uses it to help new friends stand up to a bully.
Identifiers: LCCN 2017026511| ISBN 9781512498325 (lb) | ISBN 9781541510487 (pb) | ISBN 9781512498332 (eb pdf)
Subjects: | CYAC: Psychokinesis—Fiction. | Ability—Fiction. | Bullying—Fiction. | Friendship—Fiction. | Theater—Fiction. | High schools—Fiction. | Schools—Fiction.
Classification: LCC PZ7.1.M37346 Min 2018 | DDC [Fic]—dc23

LC record available at https://lccn.loc.gov/2017026511

Manufactured in the United States of America
1-43587-33364-8/29/2017

For Dirk

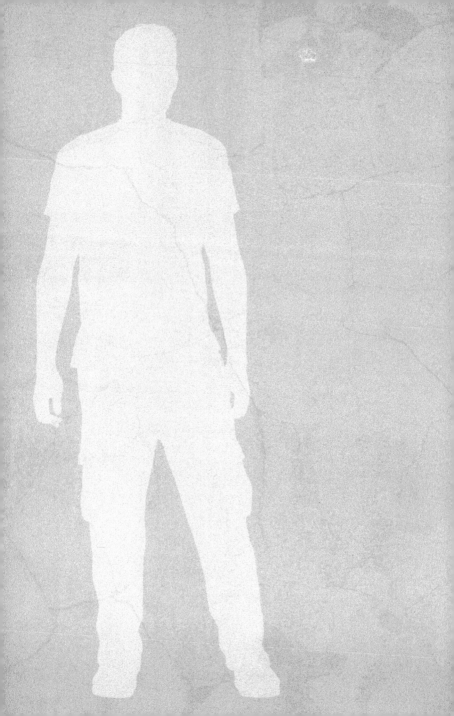

SIXTEEN YEARS AGO, ON APRIL 12, SIX PEOPLE FROM AROUND THE COUNTRY WERE BORN WITH A HIDDEN SPECIAL ABILITY.

On their sixteenth birthday, they each develop their special ability for the first time. Whether they can soar through the clouds, run faster than the speed of light, or tear through a brick wall, all the teenagers must choose how to use their powers. Will they keep their abilities secret? Will they use them only to benefit themselves? Or will they attempt to help others—even if the risks are greater than they could imagine? One way or another, each teen will have to learn what it means to be . . . superhuman.

1

"Move it!"

Parker heard the words, followed by the crash of a student getting shoved into a nearby locker. He looked over and saw MJ Mursh, a senior, laughing with his friends and walking away from where Mark Pollack, a sophomore, bent down to pick up the books he'd just dropped.

Some things never change, Parker thought to himself, walking past Mark as he headed toward the school theater. This happened nearly every day.

No one paid Parker any attention as he moved through the halls. He had trouble being noticed at all, and not just by other students. Last year, a teacher had marked him as absent for a class because simply she hadn't realized he was there.

Sometimes Parker preferred things this way. Not being noticed meant less of a chance that he'd get picked on. He'd rather stay under the radar if it meant people left him alone.

He'd had a few friends in middle school, but most of them had gone to a different high school once they all got to ninth grade, and the one or two that did come to the same school lost touch pretty quickly after they joined different clubs and sports. Nowadays, Parker tended to prefer solitary activities over social ones, and making new friends wasn't exactly in his wheelhouse, so he soon found it was easier to just keep to himself.

Then last year he signed up to work in the theater crew for the fall play just to have *something* to put on a college application. Ms. Frasier, the theater director and drama teacher, had put him to work building props because the students who did it previously had all graduated. The quiet, secluded workshop and the nature of crew members remaining behind the scenes suited him well, and Parker had signed up to work on the crew for every production since.

He was heading to the workshop now. This year's spring production was just getting started, and Parker had to build numerous set pieces—trees, bushes, benches, a rocking chair, the side of a house with a window and a door, an entire living room.

He and Ms. Frasier would go over designs for set pieces, and he would work on them in the solitude of the theater's workshop. During the actual performances, Parker, along with several other students, would wear all black clothing and move sets around between scenes. It was perfect—he could contribute without ever being seen.

The theater was empty except for Ms. Frasier sitting on the edge of the stage, facing the empty seats and reading through the script with a pen in her hand. She looked up from the pages when he entered.

"Ah, Parker, my saving grace, what would I do without you?" She was always like this, treating everyone as if they'd just pulled her from a burning building. "I've seen some of what you've built so far—*fabulous*, Parker, absolutely fabulous!"

All I've built so far is a bench, Parker thought to himself. *And it's not even painted yet.* "Thanks," he said quietly.

The door to the theater opened. Ms. Frasier waved an arm dramatically as students started walking in. "Good afternoon, everyone. Let's get started!"

He was grateful to leave the director's presence. She was nice, but sometimes she was a little . . . too much. The workshop was empty off to the left, or stage right in theater terms. Through a hallway, the door to the workshop was a sliding piece of plywood with a lock that wasn't attached to anything. Parker usually had the space to himself since he was the only person on the theater crew who built props. The other crew members worked on sound and lighting and other production jobs.

That was fine with him—the more solitude, the better. Occasionally, someone would walk by or poke their head into the workshop, but it was mostly to ask him when a prop would be ready or where a tool was. Ms. Frasier had tried to have the shop teacher oversee Parker in his projects, but Parker had quickly proved he was capable of doing nearly everything by himself. So after two productions, the shop teacher decided to take back his evenings.

Parker put his bag on a hook by the door and got to work painting the bench. He could hear the play practice going on down the hall, but he tuned it out. When he'd first started working crew, he occasionally brought in a small set of speakers to listen to music. But that started to draw more attention to the workshop than he liked, so now he stuck with headphones.

He hadn't gotten to everything he'd wanted to, but when he saw it was 5:15, he stopped what he was doing, grabbed his bag, and left through a side door so he wouldn't disturb the rehearsal. He had to be home by 6:00 for his birthday dinner.

When he came through the front door, his dog, a yellow lab named Foster, greeted him excitedly. "Hey, buddy," Parker said, scratching him behind the ear.

His dad came out from the living room. "You ready to go?" he asked. "I'm starving." They were going to Parker's favorite Greek restaurant.

"Yeah," he said. "I just have to toss my bag upstairs."

Parker, his parents, and his little sister, Jamie, got into the car and headed to the restaurant. Other than the special location, dinner was exactly like the meals they had at their house. Parker's family didn't typically make a big deal out of birthdays. It suited Parker just fine—he didn't particularly like being the center of attention, even on an occasion like this.

When they arrived back at home, Parker quietly followed his sister back into the house.

"Mom, can I watch TV downstairs?" she asked.

"Jamie," their mom said, shrugging out of her coat, "it's Parker's birthday—how about we do something as a family?"

"Board game?" their dad suggested.

Parker gritted his teeth. He really didn't mind everyone doing their own thing for the rest of the night. He'd endured enough attention today already. "I've got a paper due actually," he said. "I should get to work on it."

"You can work on it later," his dad protested. "You only get one birthday a year—and this one is your *sixteenth* birthday! Let's have some fun!"

But Parker was already shuffling out of the kitchen. "I'm already pretty tired. I'd rather just get to work and turn in early."

His parents exchanged a glance before his dad shrugged and said, "If that's what you want."

Parker went upstairs and shut himself away in his room. When he was about halfway through writing the paper for English on his laptop, he decided to take a break and grab a soda from the kitchen. As he moved to sit back down at his desk, one of his feet got hooked on the other, and he tumbled into the chair, dropping the open can right over his computer.

It should have fallen and landed right on the keyboard, spilling the drink and ruining the computer. But it didn't. Parker felt his jaw drop as he looked at the open can hanging in midair, upside down, about a foot above the desk. Parker could see the brown, bubbling cola inside. It stayed in the can as if an invisible barrier was keeping it from pouring out the open top.

He quickly moved his computer out of the way, laying it on his bed. He turned back to the can, unable to believe what he was seeing. He poked his finger into the opening and felt the sticky soda fizz around it. There was nothing holding up the can or blocking the mouth opening. What he was looking at was impossible.

2

Parker didn't know what to do. This defied physics. *Should I show Mom and Dad?* he asked himself. He stared at the can, still stuck in the air as if Parker had paused a movie.

He was focusing so hard on the can that he jumped when someone tapped on his door. The can fell to the desk where his computer had been. Soda spilled out of it, pouring all over the place. Parker quickly grabbed the can as he said, "Uh, yeah . . . come in."

His parents popped their heads in. "We just wanted to—what happened?" his mom said.

"Nothing. Just an accident," Parker replied, putting the mostly empty can back on the desk. "I'll clean it up." Once again, he considered telling them what had just happened. *But they won't believe it*, he thought. *I wouldn't have if I hadn't just seen it myself.*

"Oh. Well, we just wanted to wish you one last happy birthday before we head off to bed," his mom said.

"Thanks."

"Don't stay up too late," his dad said with a smile.

"Uh-huh, I know."

They lingered for a moment, smiling at him, as if they were hoping he'd have more to say. He knew they were just being nice, but he was still so hyped up over what happened that he couldn't wait for them to close the door already so he could get back to figuring this out.

After they finally walked away, Parker leapt out of his chair and headed downstairs to grab some paper towels. When he came back up to his room to mop up the mess, he couldn't help shooting glances at the can as if it might do something else strange. But it didn't move.

Did I imagine the whole thing? He picked up the can, turning it around in his hands, looking for something—anything—that could have allowed the can to stop while it was falling. It looked ordinary, just like all the other soda cans he'd ever held. *Maybe I can make it happen again.*

Using his index finger, he slowly started pushing the can toward the edge of the desk. It tipped and fell to the ground just like it should. Parker picked up the can and tried one more time. The can dropped. He shook his head and muttered to himself, "Of course it falls. Nothing stops in midair."

He decided to call it quits for the night, putting his books into his backpack and setting his laptop aside. After getting ready for bed, he crawled under the covers. *Nothing stops in midair,* he said to himself as he closed his eyes and drifted off to sleep.

***

The next afternoon, Parker hadn't quite shaken off the soda can incident. He was in the theater workshop sculpting a tree branch out of plaster, but his mind kept returning to the image of the can halted in place in the air. The more he thought about it, the more he had convinced himself that his mind had been playing tricks on him. That was the only logical explanation.

He had tried one more time to make the can pause in the air before he left for school that morning. He pushed it off his desk and it hit the ground with a metallic clang.

I should probably just let it go, he told himself, putting the finishing touches on some twigs at the end of the branch. The whole thing still had to be painted, and that part took the longest. He let out a sigh and looked at the clock. Rehearsal was over, and Parker decided to go home. The plaster had to dry before he could paint it anyway.

He grabbed his bag off the hook by the workshop door. He could leave through the main entrance today since the actors had already left.

But then he heard a voice.

Parker sneaked over behind one of the backstage curtains and peered around it. Two girls stood facing each other just behind the main curtain. Parker didn't think either of them could see him.

"I'm just worried for you is all." Even though he could only see the back of her, Parker knew that was Caroline. He rolled his eyes. This was typical of her. "Being the lead is hard—I would know. I've had a lead role in every show since freshman year, and to be honest, I don't want to see you get eaten alive out there. It's a *lot* of pressure, especially when you're under the spotlights and the whole school is looking at you. I'd be more than happy to take over for you if you don't want to disappoint Ms. Frasier." Caroline sounded concerned, but her real motive wasn't exactly subtle.

She was talking to Yuan, the girl who had been cast as the lead in the play. Yuan was turned in his direction, but Parker didn't think she could see him. He didn't know Yuan particularly well, but he knew Caroline. She had a reputation for thinking that she was the most talented person in whatever room she happened to walk in to. Parker was surprised to see her alone today. She usually had a group of friends—or, as Parker thought of it, followers—with her.

Yuan didn't say anything in response, so Caroline continued. "I just don't want you to get embarrassed during a performance in front of the whole school and regret it later." She casually passed a water bottle from hand to hand as she spoke.

Yuan folded her arms across her chest. "I'm not going to give it up," she said. "The role is mine. I auditioned, just like you, and earned it fair and square."

Caroline put a hand on Yuan's shoulder, and Parker easily pictured the fake concerned look on her face. Yuan looked down at Caroline's hand and shook it off. "I'm trying to do you a favor," Caroline said. "I'll take the lead, and you can have my role. It's still a good part, just not as much pressure. No one's going to judge you for giving it up. You'd be helping the show."

"Not going to happen." Yuan said firmly, shaking her head and hoisting her bag further up her shoulder. She turned to leave. For just a second, she glanced in Parker's direction, and he shrunk back a little farther.

Before Yuan could take more than a few steps, Parker saw Caroline's shoulders tense up. She was practically shaking with anger. She looked down at her water bottle and began to unscrew the cap.

Caroline followed Yuan, and Parker could see the way she pretended to stumble. "Whoops!" she yelped, thrusting the open bottle toward Yuan.

Water came shooting out toward Yuan, and Parker felt a sudden rush of adrenaline.

The water stopped in midair.

For a second, Parker thought time had frozen, with the blob of water hanging between Caroline and Yuan. But when he saw Yuan slowly move out of the way of the floating water, he knew what had happened.

3

Caroline's hand slowly lowered from where it had still been outstretched toward Yuan. Both girls stared in shock at the suspended water. "What—" Caroline wasn't able to finish the question. The sudden sound of her voice startled Parker, and the water fell to the ground with a splash.

"That was . . ." Caroline trailed off. "Well, I have to go. Make sure you practice." She gave Yuan a tight little smile as she walked away.

Did I do that? Parker wondered, still hiding just out of sight. *I must have. I'm the common factor here. I didn't imagine what happened last night. What is going on?*

Caroline left through the theater's main door behind the empty seats, while Yuan continued to stare at the space where the water had been floating just seconds ago.

Then, to his surprise, she turned right toward him. "Did you see that?"

Parker stepped back. "I didn't try to," he blurted out. Yuan looked at him in confusion. He felt his heart beating faster as his face flushed. "There was a—I didn't know—she was—I didn't mean to do it," he finally spit out, a lot louder than he intended.

Yuan's eyes went wide. "Wait, that was you? But . . . the water just froze in the air. How did you do that?"

Stupid! Parker screamed in his own head. "I have to—I have to go."

He heard Yuan call after him, but he was already halfway to the side door and had no intention of turning around.

Once he was outside, he started running. He ran almost the entire way home and came bursting through the front door out of breath.

"Hey there," his dad said from where he was lying on the living room couch with a book on his chest. "What's with you? You get chased by a dog or something?"

"No," he panted. "I was just . . . I was just, uhh—running." Lying had never been one of Parker's strengths. "I've got homework to do," he added, scratching Foster behind the ears before hurrying upstairs to his room.

The empty soda can was still sitting on his desk. Parker sat down and stared at the can. First, he tried to push it with his mind, willing it to slide along the desk. It stayed where it was. *Maybe it has to be moving to begin with*, he thought. *Maybe I can only pause things temporarily.* He used his index finger to tap it off the desk. He willed it to stop in the air using only his thoughts. It hit the ground. He picked it up and set it back on the desk. He tried it three more times and nothing changed.

His mom's voice startled him. "What are you doing in there?"

Parker looked up and saw her standing in the hallway outside his door.

"Nothing!" he said. "It's a . . . science experiment. For school." He scrambled over to the door and pulled it closed, pretending not to notice the strange look his mom was giving him. Over and over again, he knocked the can off his desk, and every time, it fell down. Before he knew it, his dad was calling that dinner was ready. He set the can aside and went downstairs.

Parker was distracted all through dinner. *Why does it only work sometimes?* he kept asking himself while his mom and dad talked with his sister. *It's happened twice now. What am I missing?*

"Parker, did you hear me?" Parker's mom brought his attention back.

"Huh?"

"I asked you how school was today."

"Oh," he said. "It was fine." It wasn't convincing, and he caught his mom give his father a concerned glance.

"Anything interesting happen?" his dad asked.

The image of the water suspended midair popped back into Parker's head. "Nope, nothing that doesn't happen every day."

His dad raised an eyebrow, but instead of pushing it, he moved the conversation back to Jamie. Parker was relieved. He finished dinner in silence and went back up to his room.

He must have knocked the can over thirty or forty times before he paused.

Am I imagining things? he wondered, leaning back in his chair. *It happened with the can and it happened with the water bottle—two separate locations, two separate objects. The only similarity is me. What am I missing?*

He was so lost in his thoughts that he didn't notice how far back he was leaning. Just as he felt the chair tipping backward, he prepared for the familiar feeling of his stomach jumping up into his chest, but it never came.

Parker waited—five seconds, ten seconds. Still no drop.

Slowly, he opened his eyes and released the tight grip his fingers were making on the armrests. The chair was still leaning backward, although it was a lot closer to horizontal than it should have been. It should have fallen, but instead it remained at a severe tilt. It was as if he'd paused a video of the chair falling backward with him in it.

Afraid to move in case that would make the chair fall, Parker held his breath. He had done it again—stopped something in midair. But could he do more? Could he make objects move too? He pictured the back of the chair and mentally started pushing it back up to its upright position. The chair began moving. Slowly but surely, it started righting itself under Parker's control. It felt like a recliner coming up from lying down. After a few seconds, the chair was right side up again.

I'm doing this, he thought. *I moved it with my mind!*

4

The whole thing was deeply unsettling to Parker. For someone who preferred to avoid attention, the idea he could do something impossible was terrifying.

Could I actually have the power to move things with my mind? he asked himself over and over again. He could feel cold sweat form on his back. His heart started racing and his hands went a little numb.

He sat on his bed and tried desperately to calm down. At least no one knew about his power—except for maybe Yuan, but she hadn't seen exactly what happened. It seemed pretty unlikely that she could've guessed what he was capable of doing. So for now, his secret was safe. And the longer he was able to keep this to himself, the more he'd be able to focus on figuring out exactly what *was* happening. Eventually his heart slowed, and he felt more relaxed.

He hadn't finished all of his homework for tomorrow, but he went to bed anyway. *I've got bigger problems than math right now.*

***

"Hey, Parker!" He heard the shout but couldn't tell where it was coming from at first. Yuan emerged from the flood of students passing between third and fourth period.

Parker focused on the books in his locker. He pretended he didn't hear or see Yuan, but she came up and tapped him on the shoulder anyway.

"We didn't get a chance to talk before you ran off yesterday," she said, excitement in her eyes. "What was the deal with that water? It was so weird. I've never seen anything like that before."

"Who knows?" Parker said, grabbing a notebook he didn't need so he wouldn't have to look at her. "Weird things happen all the time."

"Yeah, but what do you think caused it?"

"No idea." He closed his locker door. "I have to get to class."

"Oh, okay, sure," she said, looking a little disappointed. Then she gave him a small smile. "I'll see you later then."

At lunch, Parker headed to the table in the corner where he sat every day. A few other students sometimes sat farther down, but no one ever sat with him.

"Hey!" It was Yuan again. She'd popped up from her seat when Parker passed her table. "Why don't you sit with us?" She gestured to an open spot next to her and across from two boys who were playing an elaborate card game.

Parker looked at the table where he usually sat. It was empty, the way he preferred.

Yuan's eyes flicked in the direction he was looking, then focused back to him. "There's no one over there. Here, sit down. I've seen you around the theater, but I don't think we've ever officially met. I'm Yuan. You're Parker, right?"

He nodded, reluctantly taking the offered seat and wondering where she was going with all this.

"This is Cole," She gestured to the boy sitting across from her who was too immersed in the card game to notice the mention of his name. "And this is Drew." The other boy looked up and smiled.

"You ever played?" Drew asked, gesturing to the stack of cards between him and Cole. Parker shook his head. He didn't even recognize the cards. They all had pictures of landscapes or monsters on them. "It's called *Sorcerer: The Summoning*," Drew said. "You battle each other by casting these monsters." He gestured toward a row of monsters he had in front of him.

"You can also cast enchantments and spells," Cole said. "Those help your monsters or hurt the other team. It depends on the card. There are a ton of them."

"Want to play?" Drew asked.

"Um, I'll just watch," Parker said. Drew and Cole returned to their game while Yuan smiled at him and picked up her sandwich. He didn't know what else to do, so he grabbed his fork and began stirring around his mashed potatoes.

"How long have you been working crew?" Yuan asked.

"Since last year," Parker responded without looking up from his lunch.

"I've seen you around, but I didn't really know who you were."

Parker felt like he should say something, but part of his brain was telling him not to bother. He hadn't needed friends before, and he didn't want any now.

Yuan turned toward Drew and Cole. "Remember what I told you guys about what happened yesterday?" Parker's head snapped up. "Parker was there. He saw it too."

"Sounds pretty weird," Cole said, laying down a card. "What do you think happened?"

"I don't know," Parker mumbled. He saw Yuan give him a suspicious look, but she let the issue go, changing the topic to the upcoming English paper. She seemed concerned about it and the rapidly approaching due date, but Cole was confident he could finish it in just a couple of days, despite the fact that he hadn't even started yet. Parker couldn't help being amused.

He remained silent the entire time, but when there was a lull in the conversation, Drew leaned across the table, showing Parker his cards. "I'm going to show you how to beat Cole."

Soon Parker was engrossed in listening to Drew's explanation of the game—and occasional taunting of Cole. The bell came out of nowhere. Parker realized that he'd been enjoying himself—that he actually wished lunch had lasted longer.

"We play at the table outside the door right by the theater if you want to hang out after rehearsal," Drew said, gathering cards. "We usually wait for Yuan there."

"Okay," Parker said without thinking. They all said goodbye and went in separate directions.

For the rest of the day, he wavered back and forth between joining them or not. *I'm not sure right now is a good time to hang out with new people*, he thought, painting the tree in the workshop. *Not with this whole . . . telekinesis thing going on—if that's even what it is.* He smiled to himself. *On the other hand, that card game looks like fun. And as far as friends go, I could do a lot worse than these people.*

"Hey," Yuan said from the doorway. "You coming?"

He hadn't noticed the time. "Yeah, I guess I am."

Outside, Drew and Cole were right where they said they'd be, in the middle of a game. As Parker and Yuan approached, Drew said to Cole, "You don't have enough lands to cast that." Cole took the card back and put a different one in its place.

"Parker," Drew said, turning toward them. "Come here. We've got a real game going." Parker sat next to Drew, looking at his cards, while Yuan sat next to Cole and pulled out a notebook. "I don't want to cast this yet," Drew said pointing to a card with a cyclops on it. "You want to save your better cards for later." He cast a suspicious glance at Cole. "And for when your opponent is least expecting it."

"I fear nothing," Cole said flatly.

"Do either of you have a highlighter?" Yuan asked. Cole pulled one out of his bag.

Drew continued to explain the finer points of *Sorcerer: The Summoning* while Parker patiently listened. After an hour or so of watching the game, Parker felt himself relax. The others didn't seem to care that he stayed quiet, and Parker was grateful for that. He could just sit and watch the game while the others filled the silence. Eventually, he even started getting the hang of what Drew was teaching him.

"Shouldn't you play that instead?" he said, pointing to a card.

"Aha! I forgot I had that! Nice, Parker."

Just then, a strong gust of wind whipped by, and the cards lifted off the table. They would have blown all over the grass, but Parker, completely on reflex, felt himself reach out and grab them with his mind. They hung in the air, spinning slightly, just a few inches off the table.

Cole and Drew's jaws both dropped. The wind continued but the cards stayed suspended where they were. When the gust passed, Parker let the cards fall back down onto the table.

"Just like last time," Yuan murmured to herself, staring at the cards in shock. She turned to Parker. "Was that you?"

5

"I don't really know," Parker said. "It just sort of . . . happens, I guess."

Cole and Drew collected the cards and put them away, bombarding Parker with questions the whole time. They wanted all the details— when this had started, how many times it had happened before. Parker explained every incident as best as he could.

"Well, that's it then, right?" Cole remarked after Parker had finished explaining what happened with the soda can. "It kicks in when something bad is about to happen."

Parker hadn't thought about that. It was true. Every time he had stopped something midair, it had been to prevent some sort of accident or mini disaster from happening.

Before anyone else could ask him another question, Parker stood up. "Sorry, guys, I have to get home." The others watched him but didn't stop him.

"See you tomorrow?" Yuan said, giving him another one of her small, reassuring smiles.

He looked away. If he was being honest with himself, he didn't exactly want to have to talk about this with them again. "Uh, yeah, maybe."

***

Parker surprised all of them—including himself—when he sat with them at lunch the next day. They all gave him careful smiles and talked about easy topics, like last night's episode of their favorite TV show and a new video game they were all looking forward to playing.

But Drew and Cole did keep wiggling their eyebrows and staring at Yuan. Parker seriously wondered if they thought they were being subtle. Eventually Yuan quietly cleared her throat and turned to him. "So, uh, can we talk about it?"

Parker sighed. At least she'd asked him first, instead of launching straight into more speculation. "Sure."

"Forget talking about it more," Cole said, excitedly leaning in. "I wanna *see* something again!" He grabbed his plastic fork and put it between himself and Parker. "See if you can move this."

"I'm not sure it works that way," Parker said. "I mean, so far it's only kicked in if something bad was about to happen."

"Well," Drew said, "at least this is a safe way to test it and find out."

Parker had to admit Drew was right about that. Unable to think of any other reason to argue, he glanced over his shoulder to make sure no one was paying attention to their table. He wasn't surprised to see that, in fact, no one else was paying them any attention. Then he looked at the fork. He held his hand slightly above the table and opened it with his palm facing downward. He tried to feel his mind wrap around the fork. It twitched but didn't slide to Parker right away.

He took a deep breath and focused harder. He pushed a little more, feeling some kind of invisible force reach out from him and wrap around the fork. Suddenly, it was like something clicked into place, and the fork slid right under his palm. He picked it up and handed it back to Drew, who was beaming with excitement.

"Cool!" Drew said, taking back the fork. "What else can you do?"

Parker shook his head. "I'm not sure, but I don't really want to start giving demonstrations."

"Maybe you could use it to help somebody," Yuan suggested, staring off across the lunchroom at another table.

Caroline sat with a group of jocks—MJ Mursh, Devon Jones, and Paul Thornton—as well as her best friend, Jennifer Kelly. They were all laughing and joking with one another, keeping to themselves for the moment. But Parker knew that each of them had a mean streak.

MJ was always pushing younger kids around. According to rumors, Devon frequently pressured classmates into letting him copy their work. Paul was one of those class clowns who'd gone over to the dark side. As for Jennifer and Caroline, if gossip and backstabbing were competitive sports, they'd be state champions.

He watched them for a bit until he saw a meek-looking girl wearing a backpack, probably a freshman, walking by them. MJ eyed her, then elbowed Devon and Paul with a smirk. Parker was just barely able to see his foot pop out to trip her as she passed.

As the girl unknowingly walked toward MJ's foot, Parker focused on her backpack and prepared to keep it exactly where it was if the girl started to fall.

When she hit MJ's foot and should have tumbled forward, Parker used his mind to hold the backpack in place. Her feet flailed for a moment, but she stayed upright and regained her footing. She glanced around the room, clearly unsure what just happened.

MJ looked at her in shock, but she seemed just as surprised as he was. He shrugged and looked like he was apologizing to the girl. Parker knew it wasn't an innocent mistake, but the jock was playing it off that way. He even looked a little ashamed. The girl didn't say anything back to him, just scampered away, and MJ returned to laughing with the others, clearly blowing off the incident as an odd fluke.

When Parker tore his focus away from what had happened, he noticed that Yuan, Drew, and Cole were all laughing. He couldn't help but smile himself. It felt good to have helped the girl, whose lunch remained in her hands rather than on the floor.

"Awesome!" Yuan said.

"That," Cole said, staring intensely at Parker, "was the coolest thing I've ever seen."

Drew patted him on the back. "Ever wanted to be a hero?"

6

I don't really want to be a hero.

Parker was at home in his room. He had been trying to catch up on his homework since he hadn't done any the day before. But he every time he paused to check an equation or research something online for his paper, he couldn't help thinking about what happened at lunch today. *I'm not exactly cut out for this kind of thing.*

Yuan, Cole, and Drew had all been so impressed with what he could do. Parker was impressed too, but he would have preferred to watch someone else do it. The others had encouraged him to practice his ability—do more than just keep objects in place. At the time, Parker had told them he would, but he had said that mostly to get them to stop asking him about it. He had no intention of actually testing the ability.

Throughout the rest of the evening, he had entertained the idea a little more. He had to admit to himself that he was curious what he could do. He was nearly done with all his homework and he still had the empty soda can he was practicing with earlier.

Instead of tipping it off the desk this time, he held the can at the tips of his fingertips. He focused all his attention on the can and tried to tune out everything else. He pictured his mind power reaching out and wrapping around the can, holding it in place. *I did it with the backpack, and I can do it with this,* he told himself. After a few moments of staring, he opened his hand and let it drop. The can fell into his lap.

Parker sighed. *One more try. If I can't do it this time, I'm not going to bother.*

He took the can off his lap and held it in his fingertips again. He stared and let it drop.

It didn't fall immediately. It hung in the air for a brief second before it plopped into his lap again. *I did it*, Parker thought. *It wasn't much, but I did it!*

He picked up the can again, this time determined to make it hang in the air, even if only for a little bit longer.

With the can resting on his fingertips, he pictured what he wanted to happen in his mind: the can floating just where it was in front on him. He slowly lowered his hand. This time, the can didn't come with it.

A big smile crept across Parker's face. He started laughing—he didn't know how else to react. He moved his head so he could see all angles of the can.

"This is . . ." he said quietly to himself. "This is incredible!"

He reached out to touch the can, wondering what would happen. But as he lifted his hand, there was a knock on the door. The can dropped.

His dad opened the door and peered in to tell Parker he was going to bed.

The moment the door closed, Parker picked up the soda can. This time, he didn't have to focus as hard. It felt like learning how to ride a bike. Once he got the hang of it, things clicked into place more quickly.

He made the can float for a full minute before he grabbed it again. *I wonder what else I can do.*

He tossed it straight up into the air. It flew up until it nearly touched the ceiling. Just when it was going to drop back down, he grabbed it with his mind and held it. It remained suspended about a foot out of Parker's reach. "Cool," he said.

He got another idea. Rather than letting the can drop down to him, he pictured the can coming down slowly and gently into his hand. Once again he tossed it into the air. Slowly but steadily, the can descended into his palm.

For the next few hours, Parker tested the limits of what he could do. The more he practiced, the more he began to control his ability. He threw the can across the room, stopped it midflight, and made it float back to him. Actually *moving* objects with his mind was a lot more difficult than just *stopping* them, but it was kind of like working a new muscle. The more he practiced, the easier it became.

Soon he could manipulate other objects with his mind as well: pens, pencils, notebooks. He even got ambitious and lifted a lamp.

In his excitement, he got another idea. He brought Foster into his room, bringing Foster's favorite stuffed monkey with him.

Using his mind, he lifted the toy monkey and tossed it across the room. It flew through the air, but Foster snatched it between his teeth and gently placed it in Parker's lap for him to throw again.

He played this weird version of fetch with Foster for so long that he lost track of time and didn't end up going to bed until a little after one in the morning.

***

Parker woke up still exhausted, but it didn't bother him. Learning more about what he could do was worth more than a full night of sleep.

At school, he found himself looking forward to seeing his new friends. He wanted to show Yuan, Cole, and Drew what he could do, but he still had absolutely no intention of letting anyone else find out. He wanted to make sure they knew that.

"So how'd it go?" Cole asked when Parker walked up to their lunch table. "Did you practice?"

Parker put his tray down and slid into a seat. "Yeah."

Yuan got an excited look on her face. "Well, don't keep us in suspense. Show us something."

"Not here," Parker said quietly. "Too many people around. And before we go any further with this, I want you all to promise that you won't tell anyone else about it."

Yuan, Cole, and Drew all looked at one another and shrugged. "Who would we tell?" Drew asked.

"I don't know," Parker said. "Random people you wanted to impress, I guess?"

"Hey," Cole said. "I have no interest in impressing people."

Yuan snorted and rolled her eyes at him, while Drew smiled along too. Cole had been trying to keep a straight face, but he broke out into a goofy grin as well.

Even Parker couldn't help his growing smile. "Okay, but seriously, please don't tell anyone."

"You got it," Yuan said. The other two nodded in agreement.

"Okay," Parker said. "Come to my locker after school. I'll show you there."

***

When Parker left his last class and got to his locker, he found his three friends already there waiting for him. He opened his locker as Drew said, "So? What are we about to see?"

Parker looked around, once again making sure that no one was watching. He put his bag on the ground in front of the locker and opened it. "Gather around," he said, waving them toward him. They all huddled in a circle around the locker, blocking the view of anyone who happened to turn their way.

Once he was sure he was shielded, Parker looked down at his bag and used his mind power to reach out. One by one, his textbooks and notebooks floated out of his bag and arranged themselves neatly in his locker.

"I'd do more, but I don't want to attract attention," he said when he was done.

Yuan stared at Parker. "Do you realize what you can do with this?"

Parker shrugged. "Party tricks?"

Yuan looked down the hallway where Caroline was laughing with her friends. "You can stop *them*."

Parker felt his face scrunch up. "I don't think—that's not—I don't think I want to do that."

Drew leaned in. "You're the only person that can stand up to them. They won't even suspect you. I mean, who would?" The other two nodded. "You have to."

Parker was about to continue protesting, but he caught sight of MJ walking down the hall. Mark Pollack was innocently stacking books into his locker. MJ looked up from his phone, and, clearly seeing Mark, started moving a little faster.

When MJ passed the smaller kid, he purposefully bumped into him, and Mark fell into his locker. He quickly pulled himself back out and turned toward MJ. "Sorry," MJ said in a mocking tone as he kept walking.

Mark sighed and turned back to his locker, shaking his head in defeat. Parker frowned. It was like Mark was telling himself to get used to this.

"Okay," Parker said to his friends. "I'll do it."

7

He started small, with things that could easily go unnoticed. One day in chemistry, he saw Paul Thornton slide something out of his pocket—a rubber band. With the teacher's back turned, Paul used his pen as a slingshot, preparing to shoot the rubber band at a student a few desks away. He let it fly. Parker followed the projectile with his eyes. With only a slight push from his mind, it redirected, soaring to the right of its target.

Paul didn't seem to see that anything odd had happened. He probably just figured he'd aimed badly. He returned to taking notes as Parker chuckled quietly to himself.

Over the next few days, Parker made it his mission to protect people from the bullies' attacks whenever he could. People didn't fall after they'd been tripped, projectiles missed their targets nearly every time, shoelaces stayed tied.

He had to admit, it felt good to help the other students. It felt good to be a hero.

***

"You fix the school yet?" Cole said later that week, catching up to Parker in the hallway with Yuan and Drew tailing close behind.

"I wouldn't go that far," Parker replied. "I'm sticking to little things, like flying rubber bands."

Yuan smiled. "That's a good start."

"Smart too," Drew said. "It's probably best to stay under the radar."

Even though they'd been talking and eating lunch together for the past few days, Parker was still somewhat surprised when the other three lingered next to him. It was like they wanted to hang out with him even if they weren't talking about his power. Parker tried to think of something to keep the conversation going, but then the warning bell rang. They all set off toward their next classes. "Are you going to be at rehearsal?" Yuan asked Parker.

"Yeah," he said. "I mean I'll be in the workshop, but I guess I'll technically be there."

"Cool," she said. "I'll stop by and say hey."

***

In the workshop that afternoon, Parker was painting the tree, which was a lot easier now. He thought about using his mind to control the brush, but he liked painting, and it felt better to actually do something rather than just stand there and control things with his mind.

Still . . . there was no reason not to make it easier for himself. He used his ability to tilt the top of the tree toward him. Normally he would have had to use a ladder to reach the top branches, but this was easier.

He paid close attention to the door, listening carefully for the sounds of anyone walking down the hallway outside the workshop. Once or twice he heard someone and used his mind to push the tree upright again, but no one actually came in.

He was just putting the finishing touches on one of the branches when he heard the clacking of someone coming down the hall again. He tilted the tree back to a physically possible angle and pretended to brush the trunk again, even though he'd already finished that part.

The workshop door opened and Yuan came in.

"Oh," Parker said. "I was worried you were Ms. Frasier or something."

"Doing your little trick?"

Parker demonstrated tilting the tree. "It would have taken me three days to do this with a ladder. I just finished."

"It looks great," she said.

"Thanks."

"Are you free tonight?"

"I guess," Parker was wiping some paint off his hands with a rag. It had been a long time since someone asked him if he was free. *That's probably why I am*, he thought.

"Drew's older brother is playing guitar at a coffee shop tonight. Do you want to go with us?"

Parker wasn't used to being asked to go to things. For a second, he thought he should just go home like he normally would. But "Yeah, I can go to that," came out of his mouth instead.

"Awesome." Yuan pulled out her phone and had Parker give her his number so she could text him the time and address.

That night, Parker met the others at the coffee shop. Drew had neglected to mention that his brother, Trevor, was a terrible musician. Most of the songs were off-key and had sad lyrics about some unnamed girl who had rejected him.

In the middle of a song that basically consisted of Trevor wailing about how lonely he was, Yuan leaned over to Parker and quietly asked him to pass her a sugar packet for her coffee. Instead of grabbing it with his hand, Parker lifted one out of the little bowl with his mind. The top appeared to tear itself open then pour itself into Yuan's mug.

His friends started to laugh but quickly fell silent when Trevor shot them a disapproving glance.

Parker was surprised at what a good time he had with them. Most of the crowd didn't stay for the entire show, so he technically could have left at any point. But he found himself genuinely wanting to keep hanging out with Yuan, Cole, and Drew. They were funny and laid-back—so laid-back that they'd taken this whole telekinesis thing completely in stride. Parker also appreciated that they talked to him about things like games and music—ordinary stuff that had nothing to do with his mind powers.

After the show, they all told Trevor he'd been great. Outside, though, Drew turned to the others and asked, "At what point do I stop being supportive and just tell him to give up?" The other three laughed even though Drew might have meant it as a serious question.

When Parker got home, he was happy. Having friends felt good.

He was still smiling when he arrived at school the next day. Sitting at one of the long tables in the library for study hall, he chuckled to himself as he thought about Trevor's terrible set list.

Most of the students in study hall took a table to themselves. Ashley Lopez was sitting at the table closest to Parker's. Near the end of the period, she got up and left her books sitting at the table.

Devon Jones noticed immediately. The moment Ashley was out of sight, Devon popped up from his chair and strolled over to her spot. Parker wondered what he was up to.

He watched in shock as Devon casually reached into one of Ashley's folders. Devon pulled out a worksheet, folded it into quarters, and stuffed it into his back pocket. The act was so bold and casual that Parker couldn't believe what he was seeing. He'd suspected that Devon cheated in most of his classes, but actually stealing another student's work was messed up on a whole other level. Devon walked back to where he'd been sitting, picked up his things, and walked right out of the library.

When Ashley returned, she didn't notice anything had been taken. Parker was about to tell her, but the bell rang to signal the end of the period, and Ashley rushed out of the library before Parker could say anything.

His stomach twisted. *I should have stopped Devon*, he thought. His mind went blank for a second. *That was my fault. I can't hesitate next time.*

8

It took no time at all for Parker to become bolder with his ability. In his next class that day, he saw MJ prepare a spitball, chewing up a small piece of paper and using his disassembled pen as a sort of blowgun. MJ took aim at someone across the room. Parker stopped the wad of paper in midair and let it drop to the floor. MJ watched it happen with a stunned look on his face. He nudged a friend in a desk next to him, and Parker watched him try to explain what had happened.

The next morning, Parker saw Devon again in study hall. Devon had two pieces of paper in front of him: the completed worksheet he'd taken from Ashley's backpack and a blank version of the same worksheet. He was clearly copying down Ashley's answers.

This is my chance to stop him, Parker thought. *I need a plan. And I need to act fast.* After thinking for a few moments, Parker used his ability to knock down a row of books from the shelf directly behind Devon. The papers on Devon's table went flying. The librarian rushed over and started scolding Devon about being more careful with the books in the library. Meanwhile, Parker used the distraction to slowly slide both worksheets over to his table.

Parker got up to use the bathroom but stopped as he passed Ashley's table. He purposely kept his gaze down and pretended to spot the sheet of paper sitting beneath her chair.

"Hey," he said, turning to her. "I think you dropped that."

Ashley glanced below her seat and gasped. "Oh my gosh, thank you!" she whisper-shouted. "I thought I lost that, and it's due this afternoon. I must have dropped it here yesterday." She grinned up at him and thanked him again.

Parker smiled back and nodded. As he walked past a garbage can, he may or may not have thrown away a half-finished worksheet with the name "Devon Jones" written on top of it.

***

Every day, Parker practiced his ability in the workshop and at home. He was getting much better at using it. He could make objects float and move in midair. He could spin and twirl them, juggling without using his hands. At home, he was able to control a pen so well, he could write his name without ever touching the pen.

After a few days, Parker decided to take his school activism to the next level. Instead of just preventing bad things from happening, he started taking some light revenge on bullies. Suddenly Devon was mysteriously misplacing most of his homework. Paul was telling people that books kept falling out of his locker for no reason. MJ reported that at lunch his plastic forks and spoons snapped in half when he wasn't even touching them.

Yuan, Cole, and Drew all helped too. Each day at lunch, all three would discuss instances of bullying they had witnessed, and Parker would find some way for the bullies to make up for their actions. Cheat sheets fell out of books right where teachers could see them. Pens exploded in bullies' hands just as they were starting to taunt someone.

Word was getting around. People were starting to talk about the weird things that had been happening to anyone who tried to pull anything. More and more students had noticed that physically impossible things were happening around the school. There was even a rumor that the school was haunted and a ghost was taking some kind of weird revenge. That theory was Parker's favorite.

He and his friends were extremely proud of themselves.

"It's working," Drew said to the group as they were hanging around outside before school. "Devon Jones hits me with a rubber band every day in art. Since you started," he said to Parker, "I haven't been hit once. I think he's afraid of the ghost. You aren't even in that class."

"Paul Thornton has a thing for slamming my locker door shut while I'm getting things out of it," Cole said. "He's stopped doing that too."

"No one knows it's me, right?" Parker said.

"No one suspects any of us," Yuan said. "I don't think anyone even thinks it's a person doing it. One of the sophomores named the ghost Chuck though."

"Way to go, Chuck," Drew said, patting Parker on the back.

***

"How are rehearsals going?" Cole asked Yuan one afternoon when she and Parker came out of rehearsal. Drew had begun driving the four of them home after school since they were hanging out so often lately.

"The show is going to be good," Yuan replied. "It's coming along."

"Caroline still trying to take your role?" Drew asked as they piled into his beat-up car.

Yuan shrugged from the front passenger seat. "She's just being her usual charming self. She made a point of telling me that she's already learned all my lines in case I step down."

"She'd get the part if you did?"

Yuan nodded. "If I do *anything* wrong— literally anything, she corrects me right in front of Ms. Frasier."

"Does Ms. Frasier think you're doing well?" Parker asked.

"She says she does." He could hear the concern in Yuan's voice. "But every time Caroline corrects me, I get a little scared that Ms. Frasier might, you know, believe Caroline might be better for the part."

"That's Caroline trying to get in your head," Cole said.

"Well." Yuan stared out the window. "It's working."

Parker felt bad for her. He could stop all the rubber bands and spitballs he wanted, but there was only so much he could do. There

wasn't any way for him to stop Caroline
from being so cruel if she didn't actually *do*
anything.

"If this is what it's going to be like to work
with her," Yuan continued, "I'm not sure I'll
audition for the next show. She can have it."

"Ugh," Cole blurted out. "Don't let her win."

Yuan shrugged. They spent the rest of the
car ride in silence.

9

"Line up for dodgeball!" the P.E. teacher shouted as Parker and the rest of the class filed into the gym.

In the past, dodgeball had been exactly that for Parker—he dodged balls. He didn't try to throw. He didn't try to catch. He just did his best to avoid oncoming balls until he was hit or his team won. He hated every single moment of it.

The past week had been different. He didn't fear dodgeball anymore because he'd gotten remarkably good at dodging. With a little help from his ability, he had managed not to get hit once.

There had been a couple close calls. Kids on the other team had sworn the ball had curved for no reason, but Parker just shrugged and kept dodging. At one point, he'd been the last player on his team, but after slowing a ball considerably with his mind, he made a catch and saved his team from the brink of loss.

Today was no different. Parker stayed in the back, allowing stronger and bigger kids to do the throwing while he dodged. His team wasn't doing particularly well. Before long, it was down to just him and a kid named Kevin, who also solely dodged during these games.

Parker looked across the gym. Paul Thornton was picking up one of the balls, and Parker could tell from the look he was giving him that Paul was about to throw it as hard as he could straight at him. Kevin dropped back and moved away to Parker's left.

Parker knew he wouldn't have a lot of time to react. Paul wound up and hurled the ball at him.

Parker panicked. He didn't like it when *anyone* threw a ball at him, but Paul was the biggest guy in the class. If the ball hit him, it would hurt a *lot*. The moment the ball left Paul's hand, Parker gave it a little push to the left with his mind.

It worked—the ball was going nowhere near him, but time seemed to slow as he saw the horrible mistake he'd made. The ball was now flying straight toward Kevin's head. Parker tried to give it a mental push in another direction, but it didn't work, as if his ability had missed.

Kevin wasn't even going to try to dodge. His arms came up to protect his face, but at the last second, Parker pictured the ball collapsing.

BANG!

The ball popped and fell limply to the floor. The gym went silent. Everyone turned to look at Parker—everyone but Kevin, who was still bracing for impact. Paul turned to look at Parker in confusion.

Parker stayed silent and tried to look as surprised as everyone else.

The teacher came from the sidelines and picked up the flat ball, looking it over. He shrugged, then ran off the court and shouted,

"Play ball!"

Another student picked up a different ball, and Parker was actually relieved when he was hit by it.

10

"I'm not doing it anymore," Parker said firmly.
Yuan and Cole were sitting across from him
at their lunch table. Drew was next to him and
looked a little pained at Parker's declaration.
"I almost hurt someone else, and I may as well
have told everyone in that gym what I can do."

"It was a mistake," Drew said after Parker
explained what happened. "It's not like you
were *trying* to deflect the ball toward Kevin."

Parker shook his head. "I don't care. I'm
done." The whole incident had scared him.
He'd gotten too comfortable with his ability.
He'd thought he could control this power,
but until now he hadn't thought about the

possibility that he could hurt himself or someone else without meaning to.

"You've done a lot of good," Yuan offered. "We were *just* talking about how some of the bullies have toned it down because of what you've done."

"Well, that's all the good I'm going to do," Parker said sullenly.

"C'mon, man," Cole said. "You can't just stop. So you made a mistake. It's not the end of the world. You just need a little more practice controlling your ability."

"I don't want to control it," Parker said a little louder than he intended to. "To be honest I don't want it at all."

"Well, you've got it," Cole said, taking a bite out of an apple. "So I think you should use it."

"You don't get to decide that for me," Parker said. "I decide what I do, and I've decided that I'm done. No more."

"Maybe if you—" Yuan began to say, but Parker cut her off.

"No! I told you I'm not doing it anymore, so I'm not doing it anymore. That's final."

"You kind of have to," Drew piped up. "You're the only person who can do it. If you don't use . . . whatever this is, it's like knowing who committed a crime and not turning them in."

"No, it's not," Parker shot back on reflex.

"It kind of is," Yuan said quietly. "Not using what you can do for good is irresponsible."

"You don't understand what it's like to be able to do this," Parker practically shouted at his friends. "You didn't almost get Kevin beaned in the head with a dodgeball."

"People get beaned with dodgeballs all the time," Drew said, throwing his hands up in frustration.

"Whatever. It's never been my fault before." Parker crossed his arms. "It doesn't matter. I've decided."

"Well, you should re-decide," Cole said.

"Don't tell me what to do." Parker could feel his heart beating faster, anger boiling up.

"It was one mistake," Yuan said. "You don't have to make such a big decision right away. Take some time to think about this."

The calm in her voice only made Parker even angrier. What right did she have to try to calm him down? She had no idea how he felt. None of them did.

"No," Parker snapped, standing up. His chair screeched behind him. "You guys don't get a say in this. You're not my *sidekicks* or whatever. *I've* been the one helping kids in school, while you guys just get to watch and laugh. But really, you do nothing. You think this is a game? This is my life!"

All three stared up at him in shock. In the corners of his eyes, Parker even noticed a few kids from other tables staring at him.

"Parker," Yuan started, "we're just trying to help."

"Well, *don't*. I don't care what you guys have to say about it. You aren't a part of this— you never have been."

He knew the moment he said it that he didn't really mean that, but it had come out already and he was still too angry to apologize. Drew and Cole said nothing, just looked down at the table.

Yuan narrowed her eyes at him. "Fine. If that's the way you feel."

"Fine." Parker picked up his lunch tray and marched over to the empty table where he used to eat. He refused to even look at his friends for the rest of lunch.

***

Everything went back to the way it had been before Parker discovered his ability. He walked the halls unnoticed by anyone. He ate alone at lunch, went to the theater after school, and did touch-ups on his props in the solitude of the workshop.

It's better this way, he thought. *I didn't have friends before, and I was just fine. I don't need friends now. There's nothing wrong with being a loner. Especially if they're going to push me to do something I don't want to do.*

He kept telling himself that, but he knew it wasn't completely true. He missed hanging out with them. And there was a piece of him that wanted to call or text to apologize for getting so angry.

With the play's opening night approaching, the cast started doing run-throughs of the show. In between scenes, Parker and the rest of the crew had to move set pieces around just as they would do during the performances. The actors waited offstage during scene changes, so Parker had to walk past them carrying props and furniture. He tried to avoid Yuan whenever possible.

Parker noticed Yuan seemed to be quietly avoiding him too. She wasn't harsh about it, but she somehow managed to find places to wait backstage that were always on the opposite side of where he was. Knowing that she was mad at him—or worse, disappointed in him— made him feel even more guilty.

Two days before opening night, he stayed late after rehearsal to adjust the position of the door set piece onstage. By the time he'd finished and collected his backpack from the workshop, he was one of the only people left in the theater.

But just as he was about to leave, he heard Caroline's voice.

"I'm just saying . . ." Caroline trailed after Ms. Frasier, who stood onstage jotting down notes on her clipboard. "I'm worried about the show."

The director paused at that. She turned back to Caroline and arched an eyebrow. "How so?"

"I'm not trying to be mean." Caroline widened her eyes, clasping her hands behind her. Parker rolled his eyes. "But I don't think everyone's performing at the same level. I just—I can't help but notice that Yuan seems to be struggling with her character."

Parker couldn't believe Caroline would stoop this low. Everyone in the production knew Yuan was doing an amazing job—just like everyone knew Caroline wasn't really looking out for Yuan's best interests.

"We're getting really close to opening night," Caroline continued. "And I think it might help if a more experienced actor took over the lead role."

Ms. Frasier gave Caroline a long look. "Thank you for your concern, Caroline. I think Yuan is doing wonderfully. In fact, I'm excited to see her in more productions once this one ends."

Ms. Frasier turned to walk away, and Parker could see the look of panic break out across Caroline's face. She darted in front of Ms. Frasier again.

"It's just—I'm having a difficult time in my scenes with her." She flashed a shy smile that Parker could tell was entirely fake. "Again, I'm not trying to be mean. I'm just saying that I think the play could be a lot more successful if things were . . . different." Caroline looked up at Ms. Frasier as if she'd just come up with a brilliant idea. "I know all the lines. *I* could easily take over."

Ms. Frasier gave her a look Parker had never seen before. "I don't think that will be necessary," she said firmly. "If you're having trouble in the scenes with Yuan, you may consider that the problem is on your end."

Caroline's jaw clenched, and her eyes narrowed at Ms. Frasier. "I'm *not* the problem."

"Well, everything I've seen from Yuan has been spectacular. Have a good night, Caroline." Ms. Frasier gave Caroline a tight smile and walked away. The discussion was over, and Parker could see that Caroline was not happy with the result.

He had a feeling this wasn't going to be the end of it.

***

The next day, Parker had stepped out of third period to go to the bathroom when he heard Caroline's voice again. The hallways were empty, so her already loud voice carried easily. He slowed before he came around a corner, listening in.

"She was practically encouraging her to come out for more roles, Jen," Caroline groaned. "I cannot believe that girl might steal even more parts from me. This was supposed to be *my* theater!"

Parker carefully peered around the wall. Caroline was leaning against a locker while Jennifer Kelly took a drink from the water fountain. *What are they doing?* he wondered. *Just skipping class and hanging out? How often do they do this?*

"What are you going to do?" Jennifer asked.

"I'm *not* losing any stage time to *her.*" She narrowed her eyes. "I've still got a couple of days to convince Ms. Frasier to give me the lead. If she doesn't . . . I don't want to do this, but it'll be better for the play in the long run. Yuan may have to have an accident on opening night."

11

"I thought you weren't talking to us," Cole said when Parker approached him and Drew in the hall after class.

"It's important," Parker said.

Drew looked a little more concerned than Cole. "What's up?"

"It's Caroline. I heard her talking to Jennifer Kelly earlier today. She's mad that Ms. Frasier thinks Yuan's doing a good job, and I think she's worried she's going to lose more roles to her in the future."

"So?" Cole said, opening his locker and grabbing a textbook. "Caroline's always been like that."

"I think she's going to try to pull something on opening night."

"Something like what?" Drew said.

"I don't know. Something that could get Yuan hurt."

Drew and Cole's jaws clenched at that. Parker watched as they shared a look before visibly pushing aside their concern.

"What's going on?" Yuan came up behind them. She didn't bother to acknowledge that fact that Parker had avoided the three of them for the last few days.

"I think Caroline's gonna try to sabotage your performance on opening night."

Yuan's mouth dropped slightly open in surprise. "Are you sure?"

"I heard her say that she was planning to make sure you had some kind of 'accident.'"

They all stared at one another in silence for a moment.

Then Yuan said, "Why don't we talk about this over lunch?"

"Assuming you don't mind sitting with us again," added Drew. Cole nodded agreement.

Parker felt his face creep into a smile. "Yeah." The bell rang. "I'll see you guys there."

He kept his word. Instead of sitting alone, he ate with his friends that day. They avoided talking about his ability or anything related to it. It was like a little vacation from his worries. When Parker looked at the clock and saw there were only five minutes left of lunch, he blurted out, "I'm sorry I blew up at you guys the other day."

Drew shrugged. "We shouldn't have pushed so hard, and you were right, we don't know what it's like to be able to do . . ." he paused, waving a hand in Parker's direction, "that."

"We're all sorry," Yuan said. Cole nodded as she spoke.

The conversation quickly shifted to Caroline and what she might be planning.

"To be honest," Yuan said, "I can't really picture her trying to sabotage me. She's always been the kind of person who has to get what she wants. But I have trouble believing that she'd actually do anything that would hurt a performance."

"I didn't get the sense that she's worried about this show," Parker said. "I think she's worried about the next one and the one after that. She doesn't like the idea of competition for the lead roles."

"Yeah," Drew said. "That sounds like her."

"Let's see what we can find out and take it from there," Cole suggested as the bell rang.

For the rest of the day, Cole and Drew tried to find out if Caroline had anything planned, but it didn't seem as if Caroline had confided in anyone else. Parker mentally reviewed everything Caroline had done during rehearsals. Aside from her usual passive-aggressive comments and a few snide remarks, he couldn't think of anything suspicious.

Opening night was tomorrow. Parker tried to imagine how Caroline might sabotage Yuan. She could steal or damage Yuan's costume, tamper with her microphone . . . or try to physically hurt her. Parker pictured Caroline tripping Yuan onstage, or pushing her down the stairs. It seemed extreme, but it also seemed like the easiest way for Caroline to put

Yuan out of commission.

If she tries something like that, Parker thought, *maybe I can use my ability to keep Yuan safe.* But he didn't know whether he was willing to use his ability again. He was still rattled from the dodgeball incident, and he saw his power as dangerous now. What if he tried to help Yuan and instead ended up hurting her— or hurting someone else?

But if something happened to Yuan and he did nothing to stop it, would he ever be able to forgive himself?

12

That afternoon, the cast had their last rehearsal before opening night. Parker was sitting offstage, watching a scene be repeated for what had to be the fifth or sixth time. Two of the actors had been flubbing their lines, so Ms. Frasier was having them run the scene again and again to drill it into their heads. Parker didn't need to do anything for this scene, so he had to sit and watch until Ms. Frasier decided they knew the lines well enough.

Most of the other actors had taken a seat in the audience while this went on. Yuan was out there quietly chatting with another actor.

Parker decided to run back to the workshop and grab his phone out of his bag.

When he reached the workshop, he noticed the door was slightly open—which was unusual because hardly anyone else ever went in there. Parker opened the door . . . and saw Caroline inside, looking through the toolbox.

The door creaked as he pushed it all the way open. Caroline snapped upright and turned to face Parker. "Oh, hey." She smoothed her face into a calm smile.

"What are you doing in here?"

Caroline's eyes darted back and forth around the room. She cleared her throat. "I was just bored—looking around."

She had clearly been searching for something in here. Parker crossed his arms. "Can I help you find something?"

"No," she replied a little too quickly. "I'm not—I should probably get back out there." She gave a fake smile again and scurried past him.

Parker walked over to where she had been looking. The toolbox was kind of a mess, everything tossed in randomly. She could have easily taken something and Parker would have no way of knowing what it was.

He looked back toward the door. He'd just seen something he wasn't supposed to, something Caroline didn't want him to know. He was sure of it.

Parker grabbed his phone out of his bag as an uneasy feeling swelled in his chest.

By the time he got back to the stage, Caroline was already in the audience watching the scene again. Parker kept a close eye on her, but she didn't do anything else suspicious.

What were you looking for?

***

"I still don't buy it," Yuan said as they walked out of rehearsal. Parker had just told her what he'd seen. "Caroline's ego won't let her sabotage a play that she's in. Even if she's not the lead."

"Well, why else would she be in the workshop? I've done several productions now, and I've never seen her show any interest in the workshop."

Yuan shrugged. "Maybe she *was* just bored."

They arrived outside to find Drew and Cole reading comic books. "Parker's being paranoid," Yuan announced.

Cole lowered his book. "How so?"

"He saw Caroline snooping around the workshop. Now he's convinced she's going to try and mess up opening night."

"What's the worst she can do?" Cole said. "Besides, you'll be backstage during the whole performance. You can keep an eye on things and fix whatever she tries to do."

Cole had a point, but Parker wasn't so sure. "I can't watch everything all the time," he said. "I have to move set pieces around. I'm not just twiddling my thumbs back there."

Cole shrugged. "Better than nothing."

Parker sat next to them on the bench and let the issue drop. *Maybe I am just being paranoid*, he thought. He tried to convince himself that it was just his imagination, but the gnawing feeling wouldn't go away.

This is ridiculous, he thought. *Cole's right. If something goes wrong, I have to fix it.*

If he saw Caroline do something, he'd first try to stop it without his power. But if it came down to it, if the only way he could help Yuan was to use it, then he would.

If I can.

13

Parker sat with his friends at lunch the next day. The first performance was that night, only a few hours away, and Parker was a bag of nerves.

"Would you relax?" Yuan insisted. "Nothing is going to happen."

"If you say so," Parker said.

"I do. You guys are coming tonight, right?" she said to Cole and Drew. "The show starts at seven."

"Wouldn't miss it," Drew said.

Cole grinned at her. "Break a leg."

The rest of the day seemed to go too quickly and too slowly at the same time. Parker had trouble focusing on anything in class. He couldn't stop watching the clock.

That afternoon, the cast and crew sped through a final run-through. Then Parker helped put the set pieces in their correct places for the beginning of the play. After that, the actors headed off to their dressing rooms. The kids handling light and sound stayed in the tech booth, while the other crew members hung around backstage. There was nothing for Parker to do but wait for the performance to begin. He found himself fidgeting, unable to sit still and shifting from foot to foot with anticipation.

At 6:30, the doors opened, and the crowd started filing in. Parker peeked around the curtain to get a look at the audience. The auditorium was filling up quickly. It looked as if this would be a sold-out show.

Backstage, the actors had come out of the dressing rooms in costume, ready for the performance to begin. Caroline was on the other side of the stage from Parker. He watched her closely, but she just appeared to be mouthing her lines to herself. Parker didn't take his eyes off her. If she tried to pull something, he wanted to see it. Although once the show started, he knew that keeping an eye on her would be harder. There were a few scenes that she wasn't in—scenes when Parker had to focus on getting props and set pieces ready for the next scene change. He could only do so much.

The lights went down. *Please*, Parker thought. *Just let this go well.*

The show started.

14

Things were going well. Aside from one actor walking out onstage without his character's signature top hat, there hadn't been a single hiccup.

Whenever he could, Parker made sure to monitor Caroline, but he had to make sure that he did his job. *He* certainly didn't want to be the reason the show went poorly.

For the last few minutes of the first act, he actually got pretty laid-back about monitoring her. He was helping one of the actors adjust their wireless microphone pack when he realized he had no idea where Caroline was. He felt his heart skip a beat, but Yuan's next scene went off without a hitch, so he tried not to worry about it.

During intermission, Parker felt himself begin to relax. Everything had been going according to plan. Yuan was probably right— Caroline wouldn't sabotage a production she was in.

The second act started, and Parker waited behind the stage-left curtain. The two actors who had been flubbing their lines during rehearsal were on stage, but apparently all that practicing had been worth it. They were both doing fine tonight.

Parker caught something out of place on one of the prop tables—a screwdriver. He picked it up. *Did I leave this here?* he wondered. *No, I haven't needed to use a screwdriver in weeks.*

He looked around for Caroline, but she was nowhere to be found.

Someone probably needed it for something, he figured, sliding into his back pocket. He went back to watching the scene.

The lights went out, and Parker wheeled the tree offstage. Then he grabbed the rocking

chair while two other crew members lifted a
couch, and they set everything in place for the
next scene.

Parker zipped off stage before the lights
came up. Just as he did, he caught a quick
glimpse of something very wrong.

A giant wood panel above the door wobbled
slightly. It had never done that before. Parker
knew exactly how it was built—that panel was
screwed firmly to the doorframe. That was *all*
it was screwed to, but two other large panels on
either side kept it in place. If the middle panel
fell, it would fall right onto the actors, and it
was large enough to seriously injure someone.

Yuan was standing behind the closed door.
She had to enter the scene and deliver a big
monologue in just a few moments. Parker
rushed over. Maybe he could run a quick fix on
the door.

"What are you doing?" Yuan whispered.

"Hang on one second," he whispered
back, kneeling down to check the screws in
the doorframe.

"What?"

Parker didn't answer. He saw exactly what was wrong. The screws were gone—all of them. The second Yuan put any pressure on the door by opening it, the frame would shift and fall, and the giant panel would come collapsing down onto the stage. It was practically a miracle that it hadn't fallen already.

He wouldn't have time to put the screws back in. "Don't open the door," he whispered to Yuan.

"What?" she fired back in a whisper. "I *have* to open the door!"

"It's going to—" He stopped himself. There was no time to explain. He saw the panel wobble again. Caroline was on stage, and Parker could see her stealing glances at the door. She was obviously behind this. She probably thought that the doorframe would be the only thing that would fall over, disrupting Yuan's scene and throwing Yuan off her game. Caroline didn't know anything about carpentry. She couldn't have guessed that what she'd done would actually seriously injure Yuan.

Yuan's cue was coming up. There was nothing else Parker could do without delaying the scene. Instead, he focused on the panel. He needed to stop it from falling. The doorframe would definitely fall. That was a given. It would be an embarrassing accident, but it wouldn't put anyone in danger. On the other hand, if the panel fell, it could be a disaster.

Parker had never tried to manipulate something this big with his mind. When he'd built this set piece, he'd used his telekinesis to help, but he'd held the bottom with his arms. He wasn't even sure he *could* hold it in place with only his power. He tried to imagine pushing both sides of the panel, pressing it and holding it up. He was concentrating so hard he was actually sweating.

Yuan opened the door. There was an audible gasp from the audience. Just as Parker expected, the doorframe fell forward along with the door itself, landing with a loud crack. The panel wobbled back and forth. Parker strained to hold it, trying to control the wobble.

He could practically feel the weight pressing into his shoulders, but it was working. The panel stayed put.

For a moment, everyone was silent.

Then Parker heard Yuan angrily say to one of the other characters, "Some handyman you are. You said you fixed that door last month."

The audience laughed. Yuan continued the scene flawlessly while Parker took quick, sharp breaths, desperately working to keep the panel from falling.

He knew Yuan's monologue was only about two minutes long, but it felt like two hours. When she was done, the lights went down, and the actors rushed offstage.

Parker released his mental grip on the panel and let out a deep breath.

BANG!

The audience gasped again at the sound of the massive piece of wood slamming face down onto the middle of the stage. There was just a second of dead silence before they started murmuring.

Across the stage from Parker, Caroline had both hands covering her mouth. Her eyes were the size of dinner plates. She looked horrified.

That, thought Parker, *is definitely the face of someone who's guilty of sabotage.*

15

"Where are the screws?"

Caroline whipped around to face Parker as he stormed over to stand behind her offstage. "What screws?"

Parker felt his jaw clench. "I have to fix the set piece you ruined. Where are they?"

Caroline looked as if she were about to plead innocence, but something changed. Her face fell, and she looked ashamed instead. Silently, she reached into a pocket and produced about a dozen screws. Parker took them.

"Do you realize what would have happened if that panel had fallen on someone?"

Caroline's eyes drifted to the ground.

"Parker, what happened?" Ms. Frasier was quickly moving through the crew and actors, and she looked furious.

"Someone took the screws out from the door piece," Parker said flatly. He showed them to her.

"Who? Why would someone do that?"

Parker turned to Caroline. "Good question."

"Can you fix it?"

"Yeah," he said. "I'll come in early tomorrow and take care of it. It'll be ready to use again in time for the next show. This time, I'll screw it to the other panels too. This *won't* happen again." He was still looking at Caroline rather than the director.

The rest of the play was a bit awkward. The crew members removed the wooden panel and the show went on, but the set had a huge rectangular hole in the middle of it. Characters had to mime knocking on a door that wasn't there. At least no one had been hurt, though.

After the show, Parker caught up to Caroline as she headed toward the dressing room. "What do you want now?" she demanded, but she sounded more nervous than hostile.

"Listen," he said. "I could've ratted you out to Ms. Frasier, but I didn't. So I expect you to keep that in mind. Nothing like this is going to happen again, *right?*"

He wanted to make sure the point was driven home. Caroline opened her mouth to say something, then seemed to change her mind and simply nodded.

"Yuan won't have any more problems."

Caroline shook her head.

"Good."

***

After Yuan and Parker finished with postshow cleanup, they met Drew and Cole at a pizza place not far from the school.

"I think that ad-libbed line after the doorframe fell was actually the funniest part of the whole show," said Drew as they dug into their food.

"Yeah, some people in the audience clearly

thought that was just part of the script,"
Cole added. "At least until the panel came
crashing down."

"So what do people think caused that?"
Parker asked.

"Chuck strikes again," Cole said with a
smile. "Nobody knows."

"Word will get out that someone took out
the screws," Yuan said. "A couple people heard
you tell Ms. Frasier."

"Think they'll pin it on Caroline?"
Drew asked.

Yuan shrugged. "Maybe. But it doesn't
matter to me if she gets punished or not.
The important thing is that nobody got hurt.
And you know what? After everyone left,
she actually told me I did a good job, *and* she
apologized for the things she'd said. It felt
sincere too."

Cole nodded. "And it only took a
near disaster."

"Hey," Drew said, shrugging. "Whatever
makes her nicer." He looked at Parker. "How do
you feel about the fact that you used your power?"

Parker smiled. "It feels really good. If I hadn't been there . . ." He trailed off, not wanting to think about that too much.

"Does this mean you'll keep using your telekinesis for the greater good?" asked Drew.

"Maybe just not in dodgeball," Yuan added, nudging Parker playfully.

"Yeah," Parker said. He looked at his friends and smiled to himself. Even if he didn't use his power as frequently has he had been, it was good to know that if someone ever needed it, he was here to help.

FIVE YEARS LATER

THREE SUSPECTS CAPTURED AFTER BIZARRE ROBBERY

A robbery at Slade National Bank was interrupted after three male suspects held tellers at gunpoint. The suspects mysteriously seemed unable to leave the bank once they had the money. Witnesses report that, on their way out, the suspects suddenly froze in place. Once law enforcement arrived, the suspects claimed that they had been temporarily paralyzed. Witness Parker Pelham, who was in the bank lobby at the time of the attempted robbery, said, "I don't really know what happened. But I'm glad they didn't get away, and I'm glad no one got hurt."

...G A SUPERPOWER IS NOT
...HE COMIC BOOKS MAKE IT

...CK OUT ALL OF THE TITLES...

SUPER HUMAN

SERIES

...O OVER MATTER   STRETCHED TOO...
...U YOU SEE ME   STRONGHOL...
...KING UP SPEED   TAKE TO THE S...

WHAT WOULD YOU DO IF YOU WOKE UP IN A VIDEO GAME?

CHECK OUT ALL OF THE TITLES IN THE

LEVEL UP

SERIES

[ALIEN INVASION] [LABYRINTH] [POD RACER]
[REALM OF MYSTICS] [SAFE ZONE]
[THE ZEPHYR CONSPIRACY]

DAY OF DISASTER

AFTERSHOCK
BACKFIRE
BLACK BLIZZARD
DEEP FREEZE
VORTEX
WALL OF WATER

Would you survive?

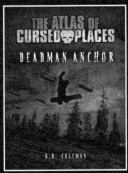

ABOUT THE AUTHOR

R. T. Martin lives in St. Paul, Minnesota. When
he is not drinking coffee or writing, he is busy
thinking about drinking coffee and writing.